I SPY

AN APPLE

For Benjamin Miles Nieves
—J.M.

For Corey and Liliana Perriello
—W.W.

Text copyright © 2011 by Jean Marzollo. Cover illustration "City Blocks" from *I Spy Fantasy* © 1994 by Walter Wick; "Nutcracker Sweets" from *I Spy Christmas* © 1992 by Walter Wick; "1, 2, 3..." from *I Spy School Days* © 1995 by Walter Wick; "View from Duck Pond Inn" from *I Spy Treasure Hunt* © 1999 by Walter Wick; "A Is for..." from *I Spy School Days* © 1995 by Walter Wick; "Storybook Theater" from *I Spy School Days* © 1995 by Walter Wick; "Masquerade" from *I Spy Mystery* © 1993 by Walter Wick; "Sand Castle" from *I Spy Fantasy* © 1994 by Walter Wick; "Blast Off!" from *I Spy Fantasy* © 1994 by Walter Wick; "1, 2, 3..." from *I Spy School Days* © 1995 by Walter Wick; "Treasure at Last!" from *I Spy Treasure Hunt* © 1999 by Walter Wick.

Library of Congress Cataloging-in-Publication Data is available.

ISBN 978-0-545-22095-8

10 9 8 7   14 15 16 17 18/0

Printed in the U.S.A. 40 • First printing, July 2011

I SPY
AN APPLE

Riddles by Jean Marzollo
Photographs by Walter Wick

SCHOLASTIC INC.

I spy

an apple,

 an orange, too,

a yellow gumdrop,

and a ribbon of blue.

I spy

a tomato,

 a yellow shoe,

a silly clown,

 and a bug that's blue.

I spy

 a yellow car,

and MAPS,

 an ice cream cone,

and two red caps.

I spy

 a bunch of bananas,

a Z,

 a little hot dog,

a horse,

 and a 3.

I spy

four yellow stars,

 a crown,

a skunk,

a spoon,

and a bunny that's brown.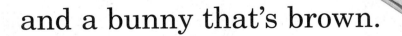

I spy

a bird,

 a mask that's blue,

a jar of glitter,

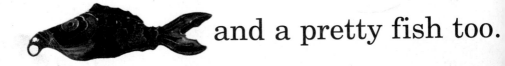 and a pretty fish too.

I spy

a sailboat,

 a surfboard that's red,

a dump truck,

a plane,

and a sandy bear head.

I spy

two whisks

with a peeler in between,

and three colored shakers:

yellow,

red,

green.

I spy

two fish,

 a pair of dice,

a golden shell,

 and a watermelon slice.

I spy

 a penny,

a dragonfly,

 a horse-head coin,

a pear,

and MY.

I spy two matching words.

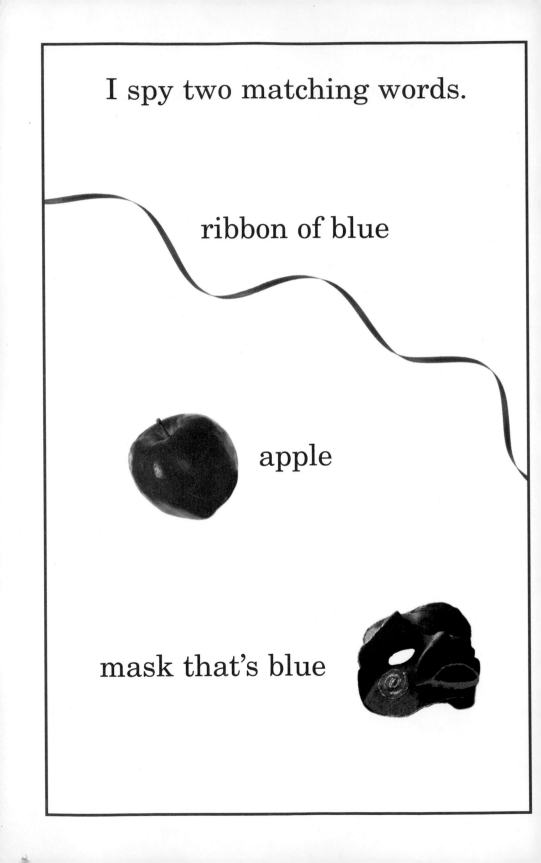

ribbon of blue

apple

mask that's blue

I spy two matching words.

two red caps

 surfboard that's red

horse

I spy four words that
start with the letter B.

bunch of bananas

 penny

bunny that's brown

I spy two words that start with the letters SH.

 tomato

golden shell

three colored shakers

I spy three words that end with the letter R.

yellow car

 jar of glitter

bug that's blue

I spy two words that end with the letters WN.

 orange

silly clown

 crown

I spy two words that rhyme.

 ice cream cone

dump truck

 watermelon slice

I spy two words that rhyme.

 sailboat

pear

 sandy bear head